To

_____

From

_____

Date

_____

Sophie

A Very Precious Angel

Sophie

A Very Precious Angel

Joanne E. De Jonge
Samuel J. Butcher, Illustrator

Baker Books

A Division of Baker Book House Co
Grand Rapids, Michigan 49516

Text copyright 1996 by Joanne E. De Jonge
Illustrations copyright 1996 by Precious Moments, Inc.

Published by Baker Books
a division of Baker Book House Company
P.O. Box 6287, Grand Rapids, MI 49516-6287

Printed in the United States of America

Library of Congress Cataloging-in-Publication Data

De Jonge, Joanne E., 1943–
    Sophie : a very precious angel / Joanne E. De Jonge ; Samuel J. Butcher, illustrator.
     p. cm.
    Summary: A young angel learns about her place in God's plan and about Jesus' mission on Earth.
    ISBN 0-8010-4135-X (cloth)
    1. Angels—Fiction. I. Butcher, Samuel J. (Samuel John), 1939– ill. II. Title. III. Title: Precious moments
PZ7.D3678So 1996
[E]—dc20   95-47611

Contents

Sophie's Diamond Dust

Sophie was a young angel, new to heaven.
She had simply appeared one day. With a flut-
ter of wings, the rustle of a robe, and a quiet

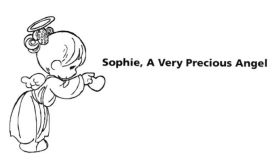

"poof," there she was. She didn't remember ever living in any other place. She didn't remember even living before she had "poofed" into heaven. God had wanted another young angel in his heavenly dwelling, the older angels told her, so he had made Sophie.

There were a few things about heaven that Sophie didn't like quite as much as most other things. Mind you, she didn't *dislike* them, because when you dislike something you're not entirely happy. And Sophie was entirely happy. But some things simply did not interest her quite as much as others.

She wasn't particularly interested in playing the harp. Not all angels play harps, you know. Sophie didn't. But she loved to sing.

She also loved to fly, to spread her shining golden wings and float on the heavenly breezes. But she never quite trusted her cloud landings. She almost feared that she would miss her footing and tumble to earth below.

There were so many things Sophie loved to do, she hardly gave harp playing or cloud perching a thought.

Sophie loved to explore. Day and night—because night is just like day in heaven—she wandered down golden streets and through heavenly houses. She danced across sparkling fields and rested by the bubbling brook where God keeps the rain before he sends it back to earth.

Sophie was not too angelic to have a little fun. She tried swinging on the pearly gates and giggled as she slid halfway down a rainbow. She also rather enjoyed climbing heavenly trees.

The other angels never frowned at Sophie. But they often said to each other, "Sophie's new here. She'll soon settle down and act like a proper angel." And they smiled at her, understandingly.

Now, this didn't quite make Sophie sad; nothing could make her sad. But it did make her feel just a little, well, not-quite-happy.

Whenever she felt like that, Sophie knew what would make her entirely happy again. She would trot off on her little angelic legs and find Jesus.

He always made her feel welcome. He would tell her that he loved her just the way she was; hadn't he helped make her that way? Then he would pat her head and help arrange her halo, and she'd feel much better again.

One day, as she was exploring a heavenly tree, Sophie slipped from a branch. Only by frantically beating her angelic wings did she save herself from a rather clumsy fall. Even she, with her limited experience as an angel, had to admit that she had not been the least bit graceful.

A group of angels hovered nearby at the time, discussing something very earnestly. Sophie flapped right through them trying to regain her balance. They, of course, said nothing, but smiled understandingly.

Sophie almost felt unhappy. At least, she felt very not-quite-happy. So she flew to find Jesus.

Nobody could imagine quite how Sophie felt when she could not find her dearest friend. Where was Jesus? She searched every house, flew over every golden street, but she couldn't find him. Jesus was not in heaven!

Downright dejected by this time, she sat on a curb, put her chubby little face in her hands, and cried.

Now, no angel had ever cried in heaven before this. Her sobs immediately brought uncounted numbers of the heavenly hosts to her side.

Stephanie, an angel who had taken Sophie under her wing when she first arrived, quietly sat down beside her. Folding her wings around the sobbing young angel she asked gently, "Can anything be wrong? Why are you crying, Sophie?"

"Where's Jesus?" Sophie blurted. "I can't find him."

"Oh, child, don't you know? Jesus has taken the form of a mortal." (Angels always call people who live on earth mortals.) "He has gone to earth."

"Earth?" Sophie couldn't believe what she heard. "Why earth? They won't love him. They don't even love each other very much."

"Oh, but he must go," Stephanie explained. "You see, Jesus loves them very much." She went

on to explain how mortals once did love God, but then decided that they loved themselves more. She explained that God wanted mortals in heaven with him, but Jesus had to go to earth and some-how make them perfect.

"We angels don't understand it completely," Stephanie finished. "But we do know that it is what God wants for mortals, so the plan is perfect."

Then Sophie did a very unangelic thing. She became almost angry, angry at mortals that they should need Jesus on earth with them and make him leave heaven. She stomped away and went to her heavenly house to brood for a while.

Of course, she wasn't really angry, because a selfish kind of anger isn't a good thing. But she was just a little put out. And, being a little put out, she thought put-out thoughts.

I wish I could talk to Jesus, she thought. *But I can't. I can't speak the mortal language yet. If only there were some way I could let him know that I miss him.*

Finally, she had an idea. *I know,* she thought. *I'll send him a message on a puff of wind. I'll blow*

ever so softly and tickle his face. Somehow he'll know it's me.

So she blew. *Just a little puff of air*, she thought, but she aimed it straight at Bethlehem. And she made the air chilly so that it would be different from the warm breezes that were blowing that night.

Can you imagine her surprise when she saw not only Bethlehem but almost all of Israel bend under a cold blast? And the blast continued until it became a full winter gale.

Did I do that? she wondered as she watched the shepherds gather their cloaks around themselves. She saw people run to their houses and close their doors against the cold. And she watched as Mary wrapped her newborn baby with a bit more cloth.

"Sophie!" Stephanie appeared at her side. "Now you know how powerful angels are. Certainly you'll think of something to help those mortals. After all, this should be the most beautiful night of all on earth. This is the night that Jesus is born."

"Oh dear," Sophie almost fretted. "I just wanted to send a message to him on earth and wasn't sure how. I'll think of something to make the night beautiful." She was very eager to prove her angelic nature.

"That's a good angel," Stephanie patted her arm. "Now I must be going. I'm part of the heavenly host assigned to bring the good news to the shepherds." With that she disappeared.

Sophie sat for a few minutes, staring into a corner of her house, wondering what to do.

"I suppose I should dust, too," she said aloud to herself.

It's a little-known fact that angels *do* dust. Little bits of diamond glitter from heaven tend to gather in the corners of their heavenly houses or mansions. Neat creatures that they are, they usually sweep up this glitter dust and throw it back into diamond glitter bins where it belongs.

Sophie had never become used to dusting. She loved the glitter, especially when it settled in the corners of her house.

It's so pretty, she thought.

That gave her a marvelous idea.

Wouldn't mortals love to see this glitter? she thought happily.

With that, she picked up a handful—for it was very thick in the corners of her house—flew to the edge of a cloud, and threw it down to earth.

"It's snowing," she heard a shepherd exclaim. "Hey, it's snowing, but look at this snow! It looks like diamond dust. It's beautiful."

Now, it had snowed on Bethlehem before that time, of course. But the snow had always been rather cold, hard rain. Sometimes it had been flakes, but that was about it. Never before had snow fallen as pure, shiny, little crystals that glittered in the light.

The shepherds could not have imagined that the snow could have been glitter dust from an angel. They thought in more earthly terms. That's why they called it diamond dust.

Sophie hardly cared what they called it. She immediately ran back to her house and gathered all the diamond glitter dust she could find, and there was a *lot* of dust. She put it into large golden bowls, flew to the edge of a cloud, and emptied the bowls completely.

The shepherds looked up again. They stared in wonder as Sophie's diamond dust floated down to earth. They smiled and even hugged each other. Shepherds usually don't hug each other.

"What a wonderful sight!" they sighed. "If only we had more light to see it."

At that very moment Stephanie and her choir of angels appeared above them. Suddenly the shepherds had light to see the beautiful gift from above, but they were afraid of these mysterious things going on.

"Fear not," Stephanie began, "for I bring you good tidings of great joy." And she went on to tell them about a more beautiful, more perfect gift from God.

Only when she finished speaking did Stephanie glance upward toward Sophie's cloud. Sophie was sure she saw Stephanie smile, not understandingly but very proudly.

So Sophie flew back to her heavenly house, serene in the fact that she had made that first Christmas a bit more beautiful. She, in her own way, had welcomed Jesus to earth.

All of this happened almost two thousand years ago. Sophie has learned a lot since then. She has come to understand the wisdom of God's plan for mortals. In fact, she has met mortals in heaven

and likes them very much. And she has learned to send messages to earth in her own Sophie-like way.

Every so often Sophie dusts her heavenly house or mansion. She always places the diamond dust in her golden bowls and sends it gently drifting to earth as fine shimmering snow. That's her way of telling us that we should welcome Jesus so that someday we can go to heaven to be with him and all love each other forever. Meanwhile, as she tosses her glittering dust to earth, she's telling us that perhaps we too can find a way to make earth a more beautiful place to live.

Sophie's Star

With a slight whisper of her wings and rustle of her robes, Sophie floated gently over a fluffy white cloud. She concentrated very hard as she

picked a likely landing spot. Then she slowly lowered herself until the soft fluff tickled her toes. Immediately she skipped to one side and sat on her knees. She gripped the edge of the cloud as she scanned the earth far below. Then she

sighed softly as she looked at the scene beneath her.

She knew that she must not go down to earth. Not yet. She was, after all, the youngest angel in heaven. She hadn't even explored all the heavenly houses yet, or wandered all the streets of gold.

And she had much to learn about the heavenly ways. Angels must learn all about heaven before they can bring bits of it to earth.

Yet she did so wish that she could make just one tiny visit to earth. Just one! Jesus, her best friend in heaven, had gone to earth, and she missed him so. Just once she would love to crawl up onto his lap and tell him how much she missed him.

But Jesus had taken the form of a mortal. (Angels always call people who live on earth mortals.) Besides that, he was just a baby mortal, small enough to fit onto *her* lap. Sophie would simply have to wait.

Sophie didn't understand what was happening. Like all angels, she didn't know God's plan for mortals. It was perfect; that she knew. But she couldn't accept it quite as serenely as older, more experienced angels. Sophie felt like she simply had to keep watching earth to see God's plan unfold.

A puzzled look crossed her face as she sorted out the scene below her. She had found the baby Jesus in a little house in Bethlehem. But nothing

was happening—nothing! Mortals nearby were treating him just like any mortal baby. No one bowed before him; no one worshiped him. No one, except his parents, paid much attention to him. Didn't mortals know who that baby was? A tiny frown creased her forehead.

"Sophie, I bring you wonderful news!"

Sophie looked heavenward, slightly startled. She hadn't heard Stephanie approach. She tried to smile at her very best angel friend, but Stephanie had seen the tiny frown.

"What's the matter, Sophie?" Stephanie interrupted her own good tidings. Then she looked toward earth.

"Oh, that," she said. "You think that Jesus should sit in a palace and every mortal should worship him? So do all the heavenly hosts, but that's not a part of the plan right now. Have patience. That's exactly what my good news is about!

"You, Sophie, have been picked to guide some mortals to worship Jesus!

"Remember the glitter dust that you sprinkled on the shepherds in Bethlehem?"

Sophie nodded, somewhat grimly. She remembered. That was the night (on earth) that Jesus was born. That was also the night that Sophie had learned what a powerful effect angels can have on earth.

"Well," Stephanie continued, "God was pleased with the way you made Bethlehem just a bit prettier with that snow. The shepherds loved it, the innkeeper loved it, and even Jesus delighted in it.

"But, as you can see below, everything is not as delightful now. Mortals have settled into their old ways. It's been only a few days, and they've forgotten Jesus. So you are to . . .

"Come away from the edge of this cloud. Sit down with me and I'll tell you all about it."

There on that fluffy white cloud Stephanie gave Sophie her very first angel assignment. Angels don't spend all their time exploring heaven. They don't even sing or play their harps continually. They certainly do praise God, but they also serve him. They do God's will in whatever way they can. They live to praise and serve God. Now Sophie had a chance to do something special to serve God.

"It is God's will that all mortals worship Jesus," Stephanie began. "The shepherds have, but not many other people have noticed him. Now some very rich, very wise foreign men are beginning to look for him. God wants the earth to know that Jesus is king over *everybody.* It is God's will that these mortals find Jesus.

"You, Sophie, are to guide them. You may not go to earth. You may not force them. God wants them to worship of their own free will. You may guide them, but don't force them. You must decide how to do that."

Then Stephanie pointed out Sophie's assignment. "Look far to the east, as mortals give direc-

tions. The men live in a strange city and a strange country far away from Jesus. See those men with their heads close together, looking at a book? Those are the men you are to guide."

Poof! Stephanie disappeared.

Sophie moved to the cloud edge again to study her mortals. They looked so different from the mortals she had been watching! Their skin color seemed darker than the mortals in

Bethlehem. Their faces seemed just a little, well, different to her. They seemed to be old, as mortals count years. And they were dressed in very strange, but rich, clothes. Nobody in Bethlehem dressed that way. Who were these foreigners? Could they really love Jesus as she did? She would just have to study them to find the answers.

But first, she told herself, *I must take one more peek at Jesus. I just want to be sure that he's still in Bethlehem.* And she leaned far over the edge of the cloud.

It just so happened that it was night in Bethlehem at this time. Sophie always had a hard time adjusting her eyes from heaven's shining brightness to earth's dull colors. Night made that much more difficult. So she leaned just a bit farther over the edge. And, without warning, she fell right off.

Now, angels usually don't fall. If they happen to trip, they spread their wings and fly. But because she was such a new angel, Sophie wasn't yet perfect in flight. So she fell.

Faster and faster she streaked toward the earth. As she tumbled, she glimpsed the dark ground of Bethlehem rising dangerously close. *Can angels hurt themselves?* she wondered in a flash.

Suddenly a huge guardian angel on his way back to heaven swooped up beneath her. He caught Sophie in his arms and gently carried her to the nearest moonbeam.

"Looks like a guardian angel to an angel," he chuckled. "No, Sophie, you will not harm yourself. But you must be more careful. Mortals might have seen you. As you fell you made quite a streak across that dark sky.

"Had those shepherds below noticed, they would have suspected an angel. As it is, your charges don't believe in angels. But you certainly caught their attention. I suggest you get back to your assignment.

"By the way," he added. "Jesus is just fine. But not many people down there know him yet."

Poof! The guardian angel disappeared.

Without a comment, Sophie zipped back to a perch above her mortals and peered down at

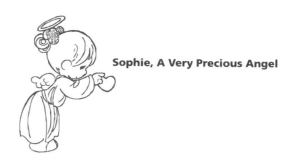

them. She was absolutely astonished at what she saw.

The men stood outside in the cold night air. Obviously they were very excited. They pointed at the sky, exactly the spot where Sophie had made her unexpected entrance. Then they put their heads together, bobbed up and down, and chattered all through each other.

Oh dear, Sophie thought. *They probably saw me. Well, at least they'll believe in angels. I'd better listen to them.*

It's a little-known fact that angels can hear every word that mortals say. They can't hear mortal thoughts, but they can hear mortal words. Angels have to concentrate because earth is so noisy. Mortal talk sounds like a constant babble to angels. But with practice, angels can sort out the sounds and listen to conversations. Especially if mortal words are directed toward heaven, angels have no trouble hearing them.

Sophie's charges were looking straight up at the sky, shouting at the tops of their voices.

"Did you see that star, Balthazzar?" one mortal cackled.

"A great portent, Melchior," the oldest croaked. "The stars are speaking to us. Something big is about to happen."

"No, no, NO! You're wrong," shouted a third mortal. "Something has happened. Two planets have come together in the sign of the fishes. You know what that means. Read the signs. A divine world ruler has appeared in Palestine. This is the beginning of the end of time! We must find this ruler."

And the rest of the mortals nodded their heads up and down.

Sophie thudded back against her cloud, amazed at what she heard. Didn't they know they had seen an angel? Didn't they care? What was all this talk about stars and planets? The "divine ruler" made sense, but nothing else did. Did they think that the stars were sending messages? What strange mortals were these?

Then an idea hit here. It flashed through her mind as brightly as she had recently flashed through the skies. *They think stars send messages. So I'll use a star to send them a message.*

Immediately she whisked herself off the cloud and into the far reaches of the heavens. She flew as far away from earth as her little angel wings would take her. Far through the corners of the universe she sailed, stopping only briefly at certain stars. Through the dark, silent reaches of space she soared, quickly at times and slowly at other times, always glancing at the stars she passed.

Finally she stopped. She had picked one of the largest, brightest stars in the heavens. She landed on it only briefly to rest. Angels often use stars as convenient, sparkling rest stops on their journeys through the heavens. Sophie had bigger plans for this star.

It's perfect, she thought. *It's so far from earth that no mortal has seen it. It's large, it's bright. They'll certainly notice this one.*

With that she slid off the far side of the star, hovered alongside it, and gave it one mighty push. Nothing happened. So she backed up a few miles, flew straight at it, and pushed again. Still nothing happened. One more time she backed up, opened her arms, flew straight at the star, and was simply stopped in midflight. She could not budge that star.

I thought angels were strong. Oh dear, and the plan was so perfect. Sophie was puzzled now.

"Where have you been, my dear friend?" a voice interrupted Sophie's thoughts. "I've been looking all over the heavens for you."

Stephanie glided to a halt in midspace. She glanced at Sophie and her star. Instantly she understood the plan.

"That's a good idea, my dear, but not quite practical. Don't you know that God placed these stars? God directs their paths through the night sky and only God can change their courses."

"You're right, of course," Sophie said. "I had almost forgotten. I was just so excited about these mortals and their stars. They watch stars. They study stars. They think stars bring messages. They even thought I . . . "

Suddenly Sophie beamed at her friend. "I've got it, Stephanie! I don't have a moment to lose. Watch this!"

Quick as a flash she sped back to the cloud above her strange charges. She glanced downward. Yes, they were still looking at the sky and arguing about the stars.

Sophie took a deep breath, clenched her fists

just a bit, and stepped off the edge of the cloud. But this time as she stepped, she unfolded her wings and soared gracefully alongside the cloud. Then she closed her eyes, concentrated very hard, and put all her energy into her thoughts.

Slowly at first, but very steadily, she began to glow. At first she glowed faintly. Then she looked like a pale moonbeam. Soon she twinkled like a little star. And then she beamed brightly. She looked like the biggest, most wonderful star any mortal had ever seen. She took every ounce of

angel energy in her body and made it into wonderful starlight.

Below her, the men looked up in amazement.

"There it is again, right above us," shouted one.

"Obviously," observed another dryly. "Certainly we must pay attention."

"Well, what are we waiting for?" asked the smallest one. "Let's go!" he screamed.

Sophie beamed inside and out. She had gotten their attention. Now all she had to do was lead them to Jesus.

"Not so fast," cautioned one. "We must pack our camels. We must prepare for a long journey. We must be sure of the message. Is this a king that we seek?"

"It's Jesus," Sophie said very quietly. The men below couldn't hear her. "You're looking for Jesus, the King of the world."

One of the men asked, "What's his name? Where does he live? Is this truly a divine ruler?"

"Jesus, Jesus. You seek Jesus," Sophie said impatiently. "If you seek him, you will find him." If only the men below could hear her. But of course they

couldn't. They didn't even believe in angels. Any mortal who doesn't believe in angels certainly isn't listening to them.

Come, come, Sophie said to herself. *Follow me. I'll guide you strange people to Jesus.* And she moved just a bit toward Bethlehem.

The strangers below almost fell over themselves.

"It's moving, it's moving. Let's go!" one shouted.

"Quick, get your camels," another one ordered.

"We need supplies. We need to bring gifts. No one goes before a king unprepared," said an older mortal who thought he was wiser than the rest of them.

Sophie had one rough moment there. She simply couldn't understand why these strange people didn't drop all and rush to see Jesus. Then she reminded herself that they were somewhat different. Yet they were seeking Jesus. She would do all she could to guide them.

Over the next few days Sophie learned a lot about angelic patience. These were very slow mortals. They had a very long journey to a very important meeting. At times it seemed they would never get going. Yet Sophie stuck to her angel assignment. Finally the group was ready to start the journey—some men and lots of camels following one (very patient) "star."

Sophie soon fell into a pattern with her charges.

By night she glowed with all the energy in her body. Slowly but surely she inched her way across the sky toward Israel. Every inch of the way she said softly, "If you seek him, you will find him. If you seek him, you will find him."

The men caught her spirit. Yes, they decided, they were seeking a divine king. They would follow their "star," find this king, and worship him. Their excitement grew as they inched their way to Israel.

By day the men rested. So did Sophie. And during this time she had a chance to study her mortals closely.

A strange but wonderful change came over Sophie as she began to understand her "strange mortals." Ever so slowly she learned that maybe they weren't so strange after all. They certainly were different from other mortals, but they were seeking Jesus. That's all that mattered.

Just as Sophie began to think that the journey would last forever (angels truly understand "forever"), it ended. They finally reached Israel.

In one last joyful surge, the little angel glowed as brightly as she ever had, right in the middle of the day. The wise men glanced at her briefly as they gathered their gifts and entered the house where Jesus stayed.

But best of all, Sophie managed one short glance into the house. There she saw Jesus smiling directly at her!

No one on earth and none of the heavenly hosts can imagine Sophie's joy. She had completed her first angel assignment! She had guided mortals to Jesus!

That day there was great rejoicing in heaven. Heaven rejoices every time a mortal is led to Jesus. This was special because Sophie, heaven's newest angel, had led them! Angels gathered around her and hugged her, and members of the angel choir sang to her.

But best of all, that very day Sophie was put in charge of the heavens. Not the stars, because only God can set their courses. Comets and meteors are different. Those Sophie now controls.

Some clear, starry night, when the heavens seem a-glitter, go outside and sit very still. Look in wonder at all the stars God has placed in the heavens. And watch carefully for a bright flash to streak among the twinkling stars. It just may be Sophie saying to you, "If you seek him, you will find him."

Sophie's Robe

Sophie missed Jesus. Oh, how she missed him!
She longed to climb up into his lap again, to sit
quietly and listen to his gentle voice. Just to know

that he was nearby, she thought, would make her feel absolutely wonderful again.

But Jesus wasn't nearby. He was on earth, and Sophie, an angel, was in heaven.

Sophie knew that Jesus had wanted to go to earth. He loved mortals. (Angels like Sophie always call people who live on earth mortals.) He wanted mortals in heaven with him. But mortals couldn't enter heaven by themselves, so Jesus had gone to earth to help them.

Because Sophie was the newest angel in heaven, she stayed right there. She had much to learn about heavenly ways before she could travel to earth.

She still stubbed her chubby toes once in a while as she walked the golden streets. When she slid down rainbows, just for the fun of it, she wasn't entirely graceful. And her cloud landings left much to be desired. She always bumped, rolled, and crash-landed, changing the shape of the cloud completely. Any angel that cannot land gently on a cloud definitely is not ready to travel to earth.

Although Sophie stayed in heaven, she could see Jesus on earth. Angels can see everything on earth. They simply perch on a cloud and peek over the edge. Trees and buildings don't bother them at all. Their angel eyes can see right through those things. So Sophie could watch Jesus at any

time. But watching him from afar wasn't quite like sitting on his lap, and she missed sitting on his lap.

On one particularly bright sunny day, Sophie decided to sit and watch Jesus on earth. She had seen him grow from a baby to a man. She sighed as she settled on a large fleecy cloud. (She always picked large clouds. She thought that a smaller cloud might break apart as she landed.) She gripped the edge of the cloud tightly as she peered down toward earth.

"If only I could be near Jesus," she said to no other angel in particular. "If I could just go to earth."

"You will, Sophie. You will."

Sophie turned to see Stephanie land gracefully behind her. Stephanie was a very wise angel who had been in heaven a long, long time. She knew all the angelic ways and was helping Sophie learn them.

"You must practice your cloud landings a bit more," Stephanie continued as she gathered Sophie under her wing. "You are becoming more graceful. You'll be ready soon."

"Ready for what?" Sophie glanced at her friend.

"Soon, I hear, you will have some practice flights to earth." Stephanie smiled serenely. "You are to become an apprentice guardian angel."

Guardian angels were not always guardian angels. They all spent some time first as apprentice guardians. That is, they guarded a mortal while an experienced guardian angel helped them. Only when they proved themselves could they become full-fledged guardian angels.

"There is a little boy in Israel named David," Stephanie continued. "His guardian angel has learned the mortal language well and soon will become a messenger angel. David will need a new guardian."

A little boy! Sophie thought that was perfect. Since she was such a young angel, she surely would understand David. And he lived in Israel. That's where Jesus lived!

Sophie stood up clapping her hands. She couldn't wait to get started.

"But wait." Stephanie held her gently. "You

must meet David's guardian angel. He'll tell you how guardian angels must behave."

With that, Stephanie disappeared and another angel took her place. He was very large, Sophie thought, and seemed oh, so kind.

"So you're Sophie, my apprentice," he said gently. "I'm Stephen. Sit down and let me tell you about David."

For several hours the two angels discussed David. Stephen told Sophie all about David's life

and what he liked to do and how he was usually good but sometimes not too good. He listed all the mortal things that could harm David, and he also told Sophie what rules guardian angels must follow.

"Just remember these two rules. One, don't let David or any other mortal see you. And, two, don't interfere with David's life unless it is absolutely necessary. Only in very special cases may guardian angels break these rules.

"Now, why don't you guard him for the next two days," Stephen finished. "I have some messages to deliver, but I'll be watching." With that he swooped to earth.

Sophie immediately settled on her cloud to watch David. She could watch him from afar, she decided. She would not interfere. Right then she was happy just knowing she had permission to visit earth.

The whole first day and night passed almost without event. Sophie saw no reason to interfere, so she stayed on her cloud. But the next day was different.

Sophie again sat on a cloud watching David. He and his mother were in a crowd of people, so she worried about him just a bit. After all, he was quite a small child.

When she saw that the crowd was going to see Jesus, Sophie decided that she simply had to go down there. After all, didn't she as an apprentice have permission to visit earth? Besides, David might be in some danger and she really did want

to be near Jesus for just a little while. So Sophie stood up on her cloud, stretched her wings, and swooped to earth.

In her excitement and her eagerness to make a graceful landing, she almost forgot one very important rule. David must not see her. She remembered just as she landed in the crowd next to her little charge. Instantly, she made herself invisible. Yet, she was almost too late. David had seen the hem of her shining white robe.

"Mommy, the sun is so bright," he said as he rubbed his eyes.

Sophie heaved a sigh of relief. At least he hadn't recognized that she was an angel. But that made Sophie a little jumpy so she immediately returned to her cloud.

"Sophie, Sophie." Stephen was waiting on her cloud. "You know that David is fine. You were eager to be near Jesus, I know, but don't let that interfere with your guarding duties. Please do be careful."

"I will, I will," Sophie promised. "I want to visit Jesus. But I will be a good guardian angel."

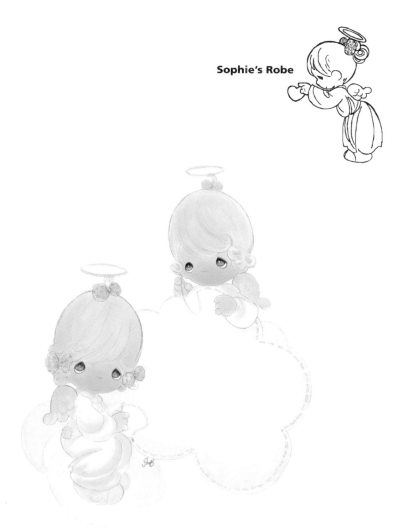

And she was. For months, whenever she was needed to guard David, Sophie was a perfect apprentice guardian angel.

When she wasn't guarding David, Sophie practiced her landings. She landed on clouds and she landed on trees. She even landed on the pearly gates. She flew in low and she flew in high. She flew swiftly and she flew slowly. Gradually, Sophie became a very graceful angel. Her cloud landings, especially, were perfect.

"Sophie, Sophie!" Stephanie called as the young angel was practicing above a cloud. "Good news! I hear in the heavenly courts that you are soon to become a full-fledged guardian angel. Stephen has become a full-time messenger angel. So you will be David's guardian."

Stephanie had been a guardian angel, so she knew the rules. She had also learned the mortal language, so she had graduated to become a messenger angel. But, once angels learn something, they never forget. So messenger angels can fill in as guardians, and they can even help apprentice guardians.

And angels love to help each other. There's never a lack of guardians to help a new apprentice. Stephanie especially wanted to help Sophie because they were such dear friends.

So it happened that Sophie and Stephanie were together on The Day. Sophie later always called it The Day—rather than just another mortal day—because it was so special.

Stephanie silently glided to a cloud high in the

heavens. Sophie perched on a lower cloud and began her guardian duties.

Again, David walked in a crowd. Sophie worried a little, but she also remembered the time she had almost broken a rule. So she stayed on the very edge of her cloud.

The crowd was going to see Jesus. Of course, Sophie wanted to go to earth to be near him. Instead, she gripped the edge of her cloud tightly to keep herself there. So tightly did she hold the cloud that the edges became crumpled and wet. A little rain even fell to earth.

Then she saw it happen. David had been standing near the front of the crowd. Suddenly he ran forward toward Jesus and started to crawl up onto his lap. A big man near Jesus reached forward roughly to pull David away.

"Oh, no," Sophie gasped. "Jesus loves children. Let David crawl onto his lap."

Maybe it is absolutely necessary for me to interfere, she thought. *Maybe David will never have another chance to sit on Jesus' lap. Maybe this will help David love Jesus.*

She hesitated. She certainly didn't want to break a guardian rule. But this was really important. Suddenly, another man grabbed David's arm and pulled him back.

70

In an instant Sophie was at David's side. No one saw her because she remembered to make herself invisible. Gently she reached back and surrounded David with her wing. No one could touch him or keep him from Jesus.

Then everything happened at once. David again ran forward to Jesus. Stephanie appeared at Sophie's side; only Sophie saw her.

"Sophie, that's not absolutely necessary," Stephanie whispered urgently. "Come back to your cloud. You've broken a rule."

But at the same time Jesus said loudly, "Let the little children come to me, and do not hinder them." He reached down and pulled David into his lap. He smoothed David's hair, looked directly at Sophie, and smiled that warm, kind smile that Sophie loved. "For the kingdom of heaven belongs to such as these," he finished.

Never in all of her angelic life had Sophie been so happy. Jesus had smiled his approval at her, and all was well. Slowly, ever so slowly, she floated back to her cloud.

"Sophie," Stephanie said. She smiled as she set-

tled next to the young angel. "You were absolutely right that time. Perhaps that's why God sends his young angels to guard children. You understand them and you want them near Jesus. You are wonderful."

Instantly, there was a crowd of angels around Sophie, singing and cheering and hugging her.

"Congratulations, Sophie." Stephen beamed. "You have more than proved yourself. You are now a full-fledged guardian angel."

"We're so happy for you," one angel said softly.

"You'll be a wonderful guardian," another added. And all the angels celebrated by singing, skipping, hopping, and dancing around Sophie.

"Not only have you become a full-fledged guardian angel," Stephanie added quietly, "you have also led a child to Jesus. You are a very special angel.

"And now I want to give you a gift I've been saving for a very special time. This is the time. This is for you, Sophie."

From under her robe Stephanie took another robe and gave it to Sophie. It was the most wonderful robe Sophie had ever seen. Not white, like robes angels usually wear, this robe was a glowing pink, with streaks of orange and lavender. It shone as beautifully as any glorious sunset.

Silently Sophie took the gift and hugged her very best angel friend. It was the perfect end of The Day.

Sophie no longer missed Jesus as she had before The Day. Because she was a guardian angel she could travel to earth. So, while Jesus lived on earth, Sophie often went to be near him.

She never let mortals see her, of course. But Jesus knew she was there, and he always smiled at her with that warm smile she loved.

And Sophie never crawled up into Jesus' lap while he was on earth. Instead, she led David and several other young mortals to Jesus. Many children sat on Jesus' lap because Sophie was there to help.

Sophie also has never worn that wonderful shining pink robe. Instead, she uses it for a very special purpose. Whenever she wants to remember The Day and she wants to remind children of Jesus' love, she spreads that robe across the sky. To any child on earth it looks like the most wonderful sunset they've ever seen.

Some evening, when the sky glows pink with streaks of orange and lavender, go outside, face the sunset, and listen. If you sit very quietly, you may be able to hear Sophie echo Jesus' words:

Sophie, A Very Precious Angel

"Let the little children come to me and do not hinder them, for the kingdom of heaven belongs to such as these."

Sophie's Song

Sophie loved to sing. She wasn't particularly
fond of playing the harp, as are some angels, but
she certainly loved to sing.

Soon after she appeared as the newest angel in heaven, Sophie had joined the angel choir. She loved to sing with the heavenly hosts because their music was, well, simply heavenly.

Actually, Sophie sang as a substitute member of the choir. Substitute members attend the practice sessions, but they don't always sing in the performances. When the angel choir is called to sing, all the substitutes gather to one side while the regular members take their places. If a regular member is absent—bringing a message to earth or serving as a guardian angel—then a substitute steps into place.

Sophie was always the first substitute to fill a place, so she was *almost* a regular member. She had only one more song to learn. When she knew that song perfectly, she would become a regular member.

Lately, Sophie had missed several rehearsals. She had become a guardian angel for David, a little mortal. (Angels call people who live on earth mortals.) David was always getting into some kind of trouble. So often, while the angel choir was practicing, Sophie was on earth helping David.

She didn't mind this. She loved her little mortal. In fact, she often helped him just a bit more than a guardian angel should.

You see, David lived in Israel. Jesus was on earth at the time, and he lived in Israel too. He had gone to help mortals come to heaven. Sophie didn't really understand that plan—no angel did—but she did miss Jesus in heaven. So, when she went to help David, she often spent a little time with Jesus too. She loved to be near him.

And she didn't worry about missing those choir practices. She often practiced the angelic music all by herself. Unlike most mortals, Sophie loved to practice. As she explored the heavenly houses or mansions, or danced lightly over fleecy clouds, or even as she rested in sparkling fields, she would sing bits of the music to herself softly.

"Glory to God, glory to God. Peace on earth," she would hum softly. Sometimes she would even forget herself and break into a song.

Now, angels certainly do break into song once in a while, but they usually make certain that they are very far from earth. Otherwise a mortal might hear them singing, and mortals may hear angel songs only on very special occasions.

One particular day, Sophie hummed very softly as she landed on a cloud close to earth. "Joy, Joy, Joy," she practiced as she peered toward Jerusalem.

David, her mortal charge, had gone to Jerusalem with his parents for Passover. The city was always very crowded at that time of year, and David was likely to wander from his parents. Sophie decided that she had better keep her eye on him.

Suddenly, Stephanie appeared at her side.

Stephanie was Sophie's best angel friend. She had been in heaven long before Sophie had appeared and was very wise. She even knew the mortal language, so she brought messages to

earth. And she had sung in the angel choir since the beginning of time.

"Checking on David again? Or are you looking for Jesus?" Stephanie asked gently as she landed next to the young angel.

"Well, both," Sophie admitted, smiling at her friend. "I know that Jesus is in Jerusalem because I saw him just a few days ago. Did you see all those

mortals waving palm branches at him and welcoming him to their city? It was wonderful, Stephanie.

"But David needs watching right now, too. He was lost in that crowd. He nearly fell out of a tree trying to get a palm branch."

"Do you think you can leave him for just a while?" Stephanie asked. "We're going to have an extra angel-choir practice."

"I hate to leave David," Sophie said hesitantly. "And I do know that last song almost perfectly."

"I know you do, dear," Stephanie answered gently. "All the angels are talking about how much you practice and how well you sing. They say that after this practice you'll probably become a regular member."

Sophie beamed.

"And they also say that the choir will be sent to sing soon," Stephanie continued. "Wouldn't it be wonderful if you could go as a regular member?"

"Oh, yes!" Sophie jumped up and clapped her chubby hands. "Where will we go? What's the special occasion?"

"We don't know," Stephanie answered serenely. "We never know until we are sent. Sophie, you know that we can't see into the future. We older angels have learned that we do what we are told and go where we're sent, and all is well. God always works his plan perfectly.

He'll tell us what we must know when it's time for us to know.

"But we do know that we have this extra practice. Come, let's go together."

"Let me check David one more time," Sophie said as she peeked over the edge of the cloud. "Oh, no! Look, Stephanie!"

In Jerusalem, a large crowd of mortals pushed and shoved through the streets. Alone in the crowd, in the middle of a street, sat David, He was lost and he was crying. Surely, he might be crushed or trampled by all the people!

"You go to David," Stephanie said quickly. "I'll tell the choir members where you are. Maybe we'll have one more practice." Stephanie disappeared.

Immediately Sophie made herself invisible and swept to David's side. Gently she surrounded him with her wings to protect him. Then she stood quietly, waiting for his parents to find him.

"It's Jesus of Nazareth," she heard a man say gruffly. "Look at him. He saved others, and now he can't even save himself."

"He deserves to die," a woman added. "He's nothing but a troublemaker."

Die? Jesus? Startled, Sophie looked toward where the mortals were pointing. Then she looked away, then back again. She couldn't bear to watch, but she felt that she must.

Jesus was there, on a little hill far from where she stood. But the crowd wasn't waving palm branches at him as it had, and he wasn't teaching them as he had. He was nailed to some rough boards, and the boards were planted like a dead tree, so that the whole crowd could see Jesus hang. Blood dripped from his hands and feet. Sophie could see that he was in a lot of pain.

They're trying to kill him! Sophie cried to herself. *They mustn't do that! Don't they know that Jesus is God's Son? Don't they know that he loves them? Why do they want to kill him? They can't kill him.*

But they could, and they did.

With a gasp Jesus said, "It is finished." And he died.

"NO! NO! NO!" Sophie screamed. Aloud this time, but to mortals her screams sounded like thunder.

Unable to move, she stood staring at Jesus' life-less form.

Mortals began moving away. The crowd disap-peared. David's parents found him and took him home.

Still, Sophie stood, unable to understand this awful thing. Then, ever so slowly, she lifted her wings and sadly flew back to heaven.

"Oh, Sophie, dear Sophie. You were there. You saw it all happen." Stephanie greeted the young angel.

Sophie said nothing. She didn't even smile at her friend. She felt as if nothing could ever make her happy again.

In fact, nothing could have made any angel happy. The news had spread quickly through the heavenly courts. The angel choir had stopped practicing. No angel wanted to sing. Their beloved Jesus was dead.

Angels walked quietly down the golden streets, wiping tears from their eyes. They spoke only in whispers. Some angels went to their houses and shut the doors. Others sat quietly on clouds, unable to understand what had happened. Mortals had killed the Son of God, and all the angels mourned.

"I'll never sing again," Sophie cried as she trudged through a sparkling field. "Never. I don't care that I missed that last practice. I don't even want to be a regular member of the angel choir. How can any angel ever sing again? Jesus is dead! Why did this happen?"

"You don't understand, do you, Sophie?"
Stephen, another angel friend, gently put a wing
around Sophie. "Stephanie asked me to find

you," he said softly. "She knows that you have been very sad these last few days. She wanted to come, but the angel choir has been called to perform. All the regular members must be there because this is the most special of occasions."

"Sing?" Sophie cried. "How can they sing?"

"I'm beginning to understand." Stephen smiled. "You will too if you do the job that has been assigned to you."

What am I to do? Sophie wondered.

"You're supposed to come with me," Stephen answered, reading her thoughts, as angels often do. "I'm going to earth to deliver a message. You are to help me."

"But I can't speak the mortal language. And I don't even want to talk to mortals right now."

"Come along," Stephen urged her. "You won't speak. You're to remain invisible. We're going to a garden near Jerusalem."

So Sophie made herself invisible, and the two angels sped to earth.

"Jesus!" Sophie blinked and stared. "Jesus!" she cried again.

Yes, it was Jesus! He stood in the garden where the two angels landed. He was alive! He smiled at Sophie, that gentle smile that she loved so much. Sophie stared, unable to move, not wanting to move.

"Come, Sophie," Stephen urged. "We have work to do. You must help me move that big stone, so that mortals can see that his tomb is empty."

Quickly Sophie and Stephen flitted over to a very large stone which covered a tomb. At the touch of their fingers the huge rock slowly rolled. Gradually it slid away from Jesus' tomb. Sophie saw that the inside of the tomb was empty. Only a few cloths marked the place where Jesus' body had lain. Of course, his body wasn't there because Jesus was alive.

Sophie burst into song. "Glory to God. He lives!" she sang. "He lives!"

"Shhh, Sophie," Stephen whispered. "Here come the mortals. They must not see you. They must see only me and hear my message."

Quickly he made himself visible to mortals and flew to the top of the stone. He sat there until the women saw him.

"Do not be afraid," he said to them. "I know that you are looking for Jesus, who was crucified. He is not here; he has risen just as he said."

Sophie could contain herself no longer. She knew that the women couldn't see her, but she simply had to break into song.

"He is risen," she sang. "He lives! He lives!"

The women understood only Stephen. He was speaking the mortal language. To them Sophie's song sounded like the most beautiful birdsong they had ever heard.

Sophie knew that she would probably never stop singing that song.

Their work finished, Sophie and Stephen quickly returned to heaven to join the angel celebration. And what a celebration it was! Never before had heaven been filled with quite that much laughter and song.

In fact, the angel choir performed for all the other heavenly hosts. That was the first time they had performed for the heavenly hosts instead of for mortals, because that was the most special of all occasions. All the other angels clapped and

shouted and danced for joy as the choir sang, "He is risen. He lives! He lives!"

Sophie immediately became a regular member of the angel choir. She had sung that song perfectly in the garden, and that was the last song she had to learn.

All of this happened nearly two thousand years ago, but the song still continues in heaven. Angels still like to celebrate the fact that Jesus rose from the dead to help mortals go to heaven.

In fact, once in a while you can hear the song on earth. If you walk outside, alone, and you hear the most beautiful birdsong you have ever heard, don't even try to look for the bird. You won't be able to find it. You see, it's Sophie settled on a nearby cloud, singing her song "He is risen. He lives! He lives!"

Sophie's Message

Sophie had a problem. She had been chosen to deliver a message to earth and she was nervous.

Now, we all know that angels are perfectly capable of bringing messages to mortals. (Angels always call people who live on earth mortals.) They can speak to large groups of mortals with never a quiver of their angelic stomachs. But Sophie wasn't so sure that she could do that, and she was nervous.

You see, Sophie was the newest angel in heaven. Oh, she was quick, as all angels are; she learned fast. She had become a guardian angel in record time. And she had joined the angelic choir—as a regular member, not just a substitute—sooner than any of the heavenly hosts had thought possible. But she just wasn't sure she was ready to deliver a message.

"I don't know mortal language well enough," she fretted. "I might say the wrong words."

"Don't worry, dear Sophie," her friend Stephanie comforted her. "You *will* say the right words. God will give you the words. You must trust him. When it's time for you to deliver that message, he will be sure that you are ready."

Sophie knew that what Stephanie said was true.

After all, Stephanie was a very old angel and very wise. Stephanie knew that God's plans were always perfect, and she had learned to trust him completely. But Sophie still had a little bit of trouble trusting when she didn't know the plan.

"Remember when Jesus went to earth shortly after you arrived in heaven?" Stephanie reminded her friend. "And I told you then that we angels didn't understand God's plan for mortals but that it was perfect?"

Sophie nodded.

"Remember when the mortals killed Jesus, and you thought that all was lost? I told you then to trust God's plan, and it all turned out beautifully. Now Jesus is alive and he's coming back to heaven."

"When? When, do you think?" Sophie interrupted eagerly. Sophie had really missed Jesus when he was away from heaven. She, more than any other angel, longed for his return.

"Soon, we think," Stephanie answered. "But that, too, we don't know. Yet we trust God. So you see, Sophie, if you can trust God for the big things, like his raising Jesus from the dead, surely you can trust him with your one little problem. Surely you'll be ready to deliver your message."

"I know." Sophie sighed. "I really know that. I just have to feel it a little bit more."

"Well, just to reassure you, I've been given the first few words of your message," Stephanie said. "They are 'Men of Galilee.'"

"What does 'Men of Galilee' mean?" Sophie asked. "Aren't they men of Israel?"

"Galilee is the part of Israel the men live in," said Stephanie. Then, with just a whisper of wings she disappeared.

"Men of Galilee!" Sophie gasped. "I'll be sent to Israel! Maybe I'll even see Jesus! Maybe this has something to do with his return to heaven. Oh dear, I really must practice. I wouldn't want to make a mistake on *that* message."

So Sophie practiced, and she practiced, and she practiced. As she walked the streets of gold she whispered, quietly so that no other angel would hear her, "Men of Galilee. Men of Galilee." At times she flew to a far distant cloud, so that no other angel would see her, and sang in her heavenly voice, "Men of Galilee. Men of Galilee." She even missed one rehearsal of the angelic choir because she had stayed in her house whispering, "Men of Galilee. Men of Galilee."

Sophie, A Very Precious Angel

Now, missing a rehearsal of the angelic choir usually isn't as dreadful as it first seems to be. There are always several angels—substitute choir members—who are willing to fill the absent angel's place. And, of course, Sophie knew all the songs of heaven perfectly. But it just happened that at that rehearsal a brand new angel was introduced.

Caleb, the newest angel, was a perfect cherub. He sat very quietly and listened in awe as the choir finished its last song. Then he smiled shyly, revealing a fat little dimple, as the angels clustered around him welcoming him to heaven. And he shuffled his chubby little feet just a bit as the choir members took him to meet the other heavenly hosts.

Sophie didn't meet Caleb immediately. She was in her house practicing "Men of Galilee. Men of Galilee." But, as time passed, she became aware that there was a new angel in heaven, an angel newer than she.

In fact, she saw Caleb in a sparkling field one time. She had quietly flown there to practice.

Caleb had come exploring, as new angels always do. Sophie just lowered her head, whispered, "Men of Galilee. Men of Galilee," and ignored Caleb.

Another time she saw Caleb by the bubbling brook where God keeps the rain before he sends it back to earth. But again she ignored him so that she could practice quietly.

With all that practicing and all that ignoring of other heavenly matters, you'd think Sophie would have become most confident of her message, at least the first part. But that wasn't the case. Instead, she became more and more nervous. In fact, if she were a mortal, it would have been said that she had a severe case of stage fright.

Sometimes now she even made mistakes. Once she said "Men of Israel." Another time she said "Women of Galilee" and gasped when she heard herself.

And her angelic stomach began to bother her. It was always aflutter. She hadn't gone to a heavenly feast since the last time she saw Stephanie. She just didn't feel like eating.

Other things also bothered her, particularly Caleb. Oh, she loved Caleb, there was no doubt about that. Angels always love each other. *But he*

is the newest angel in heaven, she thought to herself. She had always been the newest angel before he came. And she enjoyed being the newest angel. Now . . .

"Sophie, there you are!" Stephanie interrupted her thoughts. She smiled at the young angel. "I've missed you. We all have missed you. Where in heaven have you been? Have you spent all your time on this one little cloud so far from us?" The

older angel sat down close to Sophie, gently wrapping her wing around the young angel.

"Oh, Stephanie," the little angel said. One big tear found its way down her smooth little cheek. Sophie quickly brushed it aside with the sleeve of

her robe. Then she sniffled, the floodgates opened, and a torrent of words came out.

Sophie told her dear friend exactly what had been happening to her: how she was becoming more and more nervous, afraid that she wouldn't be able to deliver her message, how her stomach bothered her, how she really did love Caleb, but that she worried because now he was the newest angel in heaven and she didn't know . . .

"I understand," Stephanie interrupted quietly. Gently she reached down and adjusted Sophie's halo as she finished. "You don't know if there will be room on Jesus' lap for both of you."

"Room on Jesus' lap" may sound like strange words to us mortals. But Sophie understood immediately, and she knew that Stephanie had spoken Sophie's most private fear.

When Sophie was still the newest angel, and before Jesus had gone to earth, he had been Sophie's dearest friend in heaven. When she had first explored the streets of gold, and especially if she fell out of a heavenly tree, she would go to

Jesus for comfort. She would crawl up onto his lap, and he would hold her and tell her that he loved her just the way she was. Sophie had always loved to be near Jesus. She longed for the time when he would come back and she could crawl up onto his lap again.

But now Caleb was the newest angel. And, yes, very privately, Sophie was worried.

"Oh, my dear." Stephanie laughed gently. "So many worries. Let's take them one at a time. First, of course there will be room on Jesus' lap. He is God, isn't he? He can do anything, even hold both of you together. Jesus loves us all, Sophie. His love is big enough and wonderful enough to hold us all.

"Now, about Caleb. I know you love him, and Caleb knows it too. But you haven't done much to show him your love. What good is love when you keep it to yourself?"

"What can I do?" Sophie wondered out loud. "Fly to him and tell him I love him? He already knows that. Besides, I'm too busy right now. I must practice for my message."

"I'll leave the problem of Caleb for you to figure out," wise Stephanie answered. "But, as to that practicing, aren't you forgetting something? It seems to me that you're so busy worrying about making a mistake that you've forgotten what I said about trusting God."

"You're right, " Sophie agreed. "Maybe I should just stop worrying about the message."

"Well, dear, you won't have time to worry," Stephanie said. "At this very moment, Gabriel is on his way to help you."

"Gabriel!" Sophie whispered in awe. "Gabriel himself!"

It is a well-known fact that Gabriel is God's chief messenger angel. Often he has been sent to earth to bring important messages to us mortals. But not many mortals know that Gabriel helps other messenger angels. Even Sophie didn't know that.

But Sophie didn't have time to think about it. Suddenly Gabriel stood before her. Sophie looked up and saw the most magnificent angel she had ever seen. He stood extra-tall and shone extra-brightly. Under his arm he carried a magnificent golden trumpet. Yet he looked at Sophie with the most kindly expression she had ever seen on an angel's face.

"Come, Sophie," he said quietly. "I must tell you a few things about this message."

"But," Sophie protested, "I can't bother you. You are far too important to take time for me."

"Nonsense." Gabriel laughed softly. "You are one of God's creatures, just as I am. I love you and I will help you. Stephanie tells me that you are nervous. Let me put your mind at ease."

So that great angel sat down on the edge of a cloud with the next-to-newest angel in heaven. He told her all the important points that angels must remember when they deliver messages to mortals.

"First, you must appear as a mortal. So, make your wings invisible and change yourself to look like a man of Galilee." He helped Sophie practice that.

"Second, you must look directly at the mortals you address. Don't glance at any other invisible angels who may be nearby." And he helped her practice that.

"Finally, you must absolutely trust God to give you the right words." He couldn't help her practice that, but Sophie was learning.

"Now," Gabriel said, "because this is your first message and because you are a bit nervous, I shall go with you."

"You'll do that for me?" Sophie asked, still timid.

"Of course," Gabriel answered. "Think nothing of it. It's time. We're going to a hill outside Jerusalem. Come, let's go."

    With that the two angels stood up on a cloud, made their wings invisible, and gently floated to earth.

    Sophie had just a brief instant to glance around before she began her message. But in that instant everything was made clear to her.

    She saw Jesus rise slowly from the hill toward heaven. As he passed her, he smiled that gentle smile that she loved so much.

Then she glanced down to see a group of men staring up at the cloud through which Jesus had disappeared. Suddenly she knew what she must say. Standing close to Gabriel, she looked straight at those men.

"Men of Galilee," she said in a strong clear voice, "Why do you stand here looking into the sky? This same Jesus, who has been taken from you into heaven, will come back in the same way you have seen him go into heaven."

Every word rang out clearly. Sophie delivered her message absolutely perfectly!

Heaving a tiny sigh of relief, Sophie glanced at Gabriel. He smiled, and together they winged their way back to heaven.

No mortal on earth can imagine the joy of the heavenly hosts as they welcomed Jesus home. The angels sang and they danced and everyone enjoyed a huge heavenly feast. Sophie sang more beautifully and danced more gracefully than she had ever done before. She also ate more heartily, because her stomach felt perfectly fine.

After the feast, the angels went to Jesus one by one to personally welcome him back to heaven. But Sophie quietly slipped away.

She had noticed that Caleb was not at the feast. *Where was he?* she wondered. Perhaps he needed help.

Quietly Sophie flew over a few clouds looking for the newest angel. Then she checked the heavenly houses. Finally, as she was running lightly down a golden street, she found him.

Stranded in the tippy top of a heavenly tree, Caleb looked like he didn't quite know how to get down. His wings were held by branches, and

the little twig on which he stood swayed dangerously. Suddenly it snapped, and with a very
un-angelic bump Caleb landed at Sophie's feet.
He looked up at Sophie, and a big tear rolled
down his cheek.

"Dear Caleb," Sophie said gently, "those trees can be tricky. I fell out of that very same tree. I'll show you the best way down later. But now I

know exactly what will make you feel better.
Come, I'll take you to Jesus."

"You'll do that for me?" Caleb asked softly.

"Of course," Sophie said. "I love you and I will help you. Think nothing of it." With that she took the newest angel in heaven by the hand and led him to Jesus.

Without hesitation the chubby little cherub climbed right up onto Jesus' lap. Jesus smiled at him, then turned to Sophie. Eagerly, Sophie crawled up onto his lap too, because, of course, there was room for both of them.

Since that time Sophie and Caleb have become very special angel friends. Sophie helps Caleb learn the heavenly ways. That's how she shows him that she loves him.

Sophie has also delivered several messages to earth. She has never been nervous again, because she has learned to trust God.

127

Sophie, A Very Precious Angel

In fact, sometimes Sophie brings us mortals a very special message. You can hear it only if you sit under a tree alone when warm breezes blow. Some mortals say that the sound is wind rustling the leaves. But it's likely to be Sophie saying, "He is coming again. He is coming again."

Sometimes a little patch of sunlight seems to shine in your eyes as the leaves sway in the breeze. That could be Sophie, reminding you to trust God and to pass on his love to others by helping them.